THE ADVENTU...

AVERY ANN

LEAH JOCELYN MACKENZIE

Illustrated by Justin Smelser and Perrine Solara

LJ MacKenzie
Writing Décor

Dedicated with love to Vance and Vivian.
I am so blessed to have such an amazing nephew and niece.
Thanks for bringing out my inner child.

Leah Jocelyn MacKenzie wishes to thank the following people:

I experienced "it takes a village" to publish a book and there are many people I want to thank for their contribution to *The Adventures of Avery Ann*: Mom & Tom, Dad & Mo Mom, Cody, Jen & the "V's", Gail Rudisill, Jenny Morrison, Skye Wolf MacGregor, Susie Ten Eyck-Johnson and Ron & Apollo Johnson, Clare Trapp, Tara Riley Snyder, Cynthia Slon, Jessica Cramer, Kiko Flennaugh, Becky Bauer & Dave Griffith, Liz Overstreet, Hadas Gabai, Jackie & Adeline Crowell, Jocelyn, Kai & Zoe Szmidt, Stephanie, Gabbie & Bella Silverman, Janet Silverman & Anjali McRae, Jackie & Michael Young, Dee Robertson Phillips and Carolyn, Quinn & Lily Phillips, Liz Burns & CARES NW, Shauneen, Brian & Allie Doyle, Marianne Monson, Erica Roslund & Roger Shadel, John Ellis, Caius Matthews, Sean Cahill, my lawyer Kohel Haver, and my furry love, Blue. I feel so grateful and blessed to have partnered, and shared this adventure with, the amazing illustration team of Justin Smelser & Perrine Solara…"Thanks for the happy tears!"

"Three more minutes in the bathtub," says Mom.

"Okay!" Avery Ann calls back, splashing in her mask, snorkel and fins set. She pulls the stopper and the water starts swirling down the drain.

Noticing her charm bracelet is missing, she looks for it just as it slips out of sight. "Oh, No! The charm bracelet Grandma gave me is gone," says Avery Ann to Butterfly Blue, her trusty sidekick.

With a wink and a nod Butterfly Blue whispers, "Let's go get it, Blondie."

2

Avery Ann spirals down the bathtub drain, slides through the pipes, flips in the air, and dives into the open arms of the ocean, chasing her charm bracelet.

Following behind, Butterfly Blue calls, "Wait for me!"

3

Avery Ann paddles through the waves, and soon swims into a pod of dolphins. "Have you seen my charm bracelet?" she asks.

"We haven't," they say, as two of them scoop her up for a closer look. Riding in and out of the waves, Avery Ann laughs at the soft sprays of the water dancing on her face.

4

When they come to a stop, so does Avery Ann's laughter. A blowfish swims over and asks, "What is wrong, honey?"

"I lost my charm bracelet in the water," says Avery Ann.

The blowfish sounds a horn for attention. "Has anyone seen Avery Ann's charm bracelet?"

"I can take you into tight places where your bracelet might be," says a sea horse. Avery Ann climbs on and the sea horses zip away in a cloud of sand. Hanging on for the wild ride, Avery Ann zigzags over the tropical sea floor searching for her charm bracelet.

6

A stingray swims by. "Can I help, sweetie?" Avery Ann waves goodbye to the sea horses. Surfing on the stingray, she has a sweeping view of the ocean. Together they glide between gigantic rocks and schools of exotic fish, looking for a gold sparkle.

Riding into the mouth of a cave, Butterfly Blue sees gleaming teeth waiting to bite. "Look out, Avery Ann!" They quickly spin out of the cave and continue on their way.

8

With the ride over and her charm bracelet still missing, Avery Ann says farewell to the stingray and lets the current carry her into a group of sea anemones. Feeling her concern, they tickle her with their soft, wavy, outstretched tentacles, making her giggle.

At the sound of her laughter, clown fish swim over. Avery Ann asks the group for help in finding her charm bracelet. The clown fish tell her, "We heard the lobsters found something shiny."

"Thanks," says a hopeful Avery Ann.

10

On the way, a school of hammerhead sharks circle her. "To pass by, you must play a game with us."

She eyes their sharp teeth and fins nervously. "I like cards," says Avery Ann.

11

"Do you have a ten?" one shark asks.

Avery Ann grins and says, "Go fish." Five rounds later, she lays down her matching foursome, showing who is the card shark of the game. Swimming away, the sharks agree to look for her missing charm bracelet.

Next, a Kung Fu octopus floats by. Feeling feisty, Avery Ann challenges him to spar. Avery Ann defends jabs with her left arm and kicks with her right leg.

13

A puff of black ink oozes from her eight-armed challenger, who pretends to be injured. Avery Ann is declared the Martial Arts Champ as her sparring partner bows in defeat. "Do you know where I can find the lobsters?" asks Avery Ann.

"They live that way," says the Kung Fu octopus. "Be careful of their claws, Avery Ann."

14

The mermaids swim over to celebrate the Kung Fu victory by hosting a luau. Avery Ann Hula dances with her new girlfriends. The group sways their arms and hips to the right, then they sway their arms and hips to the left, moving in time with the ukulele music.

Avery Ann, with her bright smile, cute pigtails and elegant sway, is crowned Miss Hula as Butterfly Blue cheers.

Hearing the music, the Vibrant Reefers rock band joins the party. Jellyfish plays drums, shrimp is on the keyboard, starfish rocks the bass guitar, and an angelfish with a heavenly voice sings the lead.

"Want to play the electric guitar?" they ask Avery Ann.

"Yes!" Avery Ann screams. The band plays a gig for her new sea friends and Avery Ann, jamming on her six strings, cranks out hot licks to her heart's desire.

17

As the concert ends, Butterfly Blue reminds Avery Ann that bedtime is nearing. Remembering her charm bracelet, Avery Ann asks, "How far away do the lobsters live?"

"A little past the next coral reef," says the angelfish.

Avery Ann blows goodbye kisses to her friends as she swims off. "Watch out for sharp claws!" the starfish warns her.

18

Swimming into a village, Avery Ann drifts towards a large, tribal lobster. Her heart races as his shelled followers surround her, and he slowly opens his giant claw.

19

"We were told this is yours," says the leader with a smile.

Avery Ann shouts with glee, "My charm bracelet!" She lifts the beautifully beaded string from his claw carefully, and the village erupts in squeals of joy.

"We're out of here," says Butterfly Blue.

A happy Avery Ann thanks the lobsters and swims to the surface, bobbing with a family of turtles. Butterfly Blue whispers, "Time to go, Blondie!"

21

In a blink of an eye, she spills out of the faucet and back into the bathtub with Butterfly Blue by her side.

Her mom wraps Avery Ann in a towel, tugs on pajamas, and tucks her into bed. With the charm bracelet safely around her wrist, Avery Ann slips into her dreamtime adventures.

Illustrator: Justin Smelser

 I was born in Wyoming and spent most of my childhood living on working ranches throughout the western states. For the last 20 years I have called Portland, OR home. The Pacific Northwest is the perfect place to live for an avid outdoorsman like me who enjoys golfing, snowboarding, hiking, and biking. I have always had a passion for art and I am interested in many different styles and mediums. Although I have attended some college, most of my education has been through life experiences and adventures. I am looking forward to continuing my schooling in the arts as I am also changing my career path.

It has been an incredible thrill to work on this book and be a part of this creative endeavor. This project has enabled me to follow a dream and I thank Leah for this opportunity.

https://www.facebook.com/#!/pages/Justin-Smelser-Artist-Illustrator/147317508701106

Illustrator: Perrine Solara

I grew up in Oregon, spending most of my time outdoors riding and showing my two Arabian horses and spending time with my dog Keeta, a Bouvier des Flandres. In high school art class I explored my artistic abilities by drawing and painting my favorite subject- horses. I later received a BS in Animal Science from Oregon State University.

After college, I spent several years in the corporate world, the majority of it as a pharmaceutical sales representative. With mixed emotions I started off in a new direction a few years ago and became a Certified Yoga Instructor and Reiki Master. I am so happy I took that scary first step towards a career change. Now I am a facilitative healer and on a path that helps both people and animals achieve physical, emotional, and energetic balance. I have also found a renewed interest in artistic endeavors, something that had been dormant for almost 20 years.

It has been an honor to be part of this book project in so many ways, and I have learned a tremendous amount. I hope the story and drawings inspire children and adults to follow their inner adventurer and to never stop dreaming!

https://www.facebook.com/#!/pages/Perrine-Solara-Yoga-and-Healing-Practice/146406258765827

https://twitter.com/SolaraHealing

Fun Facts Bonus Section

We hope your family is inspired by and enjoyed *The Adventures of Avery Ann.*

Perrine, Justin and I thought it would be neat for the kids to read up on the sea animals portrayed as characters in this story. I hope the kid's illustrations touch your heart like they did mine.

Blessings,
Leah Jocelyn MacKenzie

Writing Décor

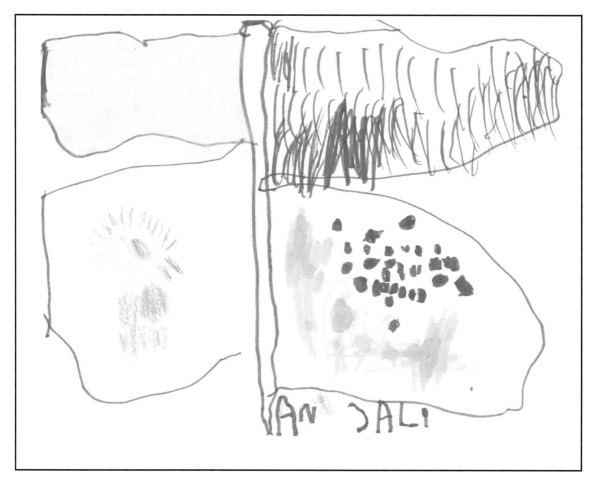

Butterfly drawn by Anjali McRae, age 5

Butterfly fun facts:

Butterflies are insects. A caterpillar turns into a butterfly. Adult butterflies have four wings that are covered with millions of tiny scales. An adult butterfly has six legs. Butterflies sip nectar from flowers for food.

Dolphin drawn by Caius Matthews, age 7

Dolphin fun facts:

Dolphins are marine mammals. Dolphins mostly eat fish and squid. Dolphins are known as one of the smartest animals. Dolphins have excellent eyesight, in and out of the water.

Blowfish drawn by Adeline Crowell, age 4

Blowfish fun facts:

Blowfish are also known as Pufferfish. Blowfish are slow, poor swimmers. To defend themselves, they swallow a lot of water to turn themselves into a large ball several times their normal size. Blowfish are poisonous.

Sea horse drawn by Apollo Johnson, age 8

Sea horse fun facts:

Male sea horses give birth to their young. Sea horses have no teeth or stomachs. Sea horses must eat almost all the time to stay alive. Sea horses can eat 3,000 or more brine shrimp a day.

Stingray drawn by Lily Phillips, age 6

Stingray fun facts:

Stingrays spend most of their time covered in the sand. The end of the stingray's tail is poisonous and used only for protection. A stingray's eyes are at their side, while its mouth, nostrils and gill slits are underneath its belly. Stingrays are known to be friendly and not afraid to swim close to divers, snorkelers or swimmers.

Sea anemone drawn by Apollo Johnson, age 8

Sea anemone fun facts:

Sea anemones spend most of their time attached to rocks on the sea floor or on coral reefs. Sea anemones sting their food with their poison-filled tentacles and then the tentacles move the food to their mouth. Some species of sea anemones can live more than 50 years.

Clown fish drawn by Gabbie Silverman, age 4

Clown fish fun facts:

Clown fish are friends with sea anemones. Clown fish live in the tentacles of sea anemones. Mucus on a clown fish's skin protects it from the poison of the sea anemone's tentacles. Clown fish keep the tentacles of the sea anemone clean and the sea anemone protects the clown fish from danger with their poisonous tentacles.

Lobster drawn by Caius Matthews, age 7

Lobster fun facts:

Lobsters have ten legs. Lobsters are related to crabs and shrimp. Lobsters live on the bottom of the ocean. Lobsters can't see very well, yet they have a good sense of taste and smell. Lobsters mostly eat fish and mollusks.

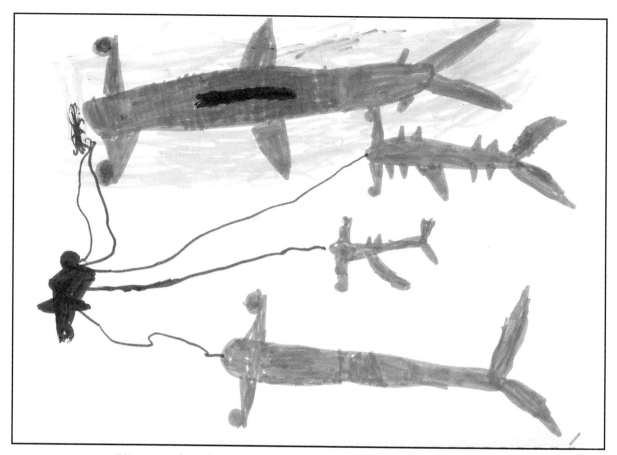

Hammerhead sharks drawn by Caius Matthews, age 7

Hammerhead sharks fun facts:

Hammerhead sharks have eyes on the sides of their head. Hammerhead sharks have a mallet-shaped head to help them scan the ocean for food. Hammerhead sharks are good hunters. Hammerhead sharks eat smaller fish, stingrays, octopus and squid.

Octopus drawn by Zoe Ryan Szmidt, age 7

Octopus fun facts:

An octopus can change its colors to match the area where it is resting, making it hard to see. An octopus blinds its attacker by releasing a cloud of black ink, giving it time to swim away. An octopus is a fast swimmer. An octopus has a soft body that can squeeze into small places to hide. An octopus has eight arms. An octopus can lose an arm and it will grow back. An octopus eats crabs, crayfish and mollusks.

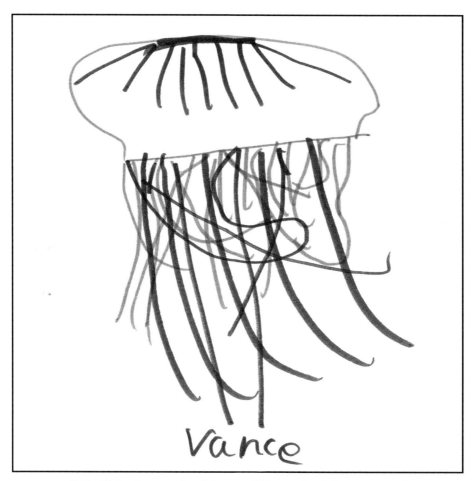

Jellyfish drawn by Vance Silver Atchison, age 6

Jellyfish fun facts:

Jellyfish have a poisonous sting. Jellyfish are pale blue and transparent, or see through, in color. Jellyfish tentacles can grow up to ten feet.

Shrimp drawn by Quinn Phillips, age 4

Shrimp fun facts:

Shrimp have ten legs. Shrimp walk around on the ocean floor. Shrimp can swim and they use their tail to steer. A female shrimp carries her eggs until they hatch. Shrimp live in oceans all over the world.

Starfish drawn by Bella Silverman, age 6

Starfish fun facts:

Starfish have no brains. Starfish have no blood. Their bodies use filtered seawater instead of blood. Most starfish have five arms. There are some rare ones that have ten, twenty, or even forty arms. Starfish are able to grow an arm back if hurt.

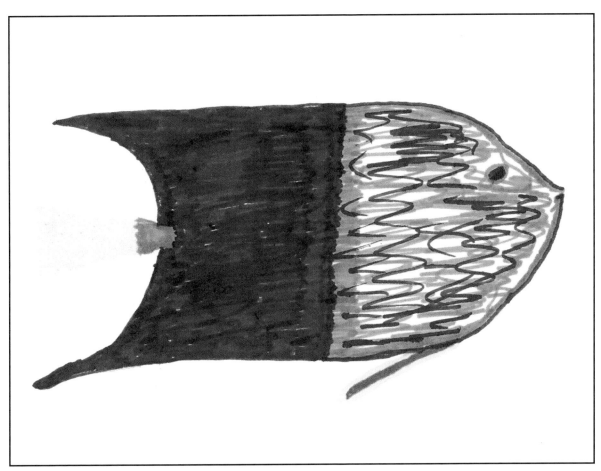

Angelfish drawn by Avery Ann, age 9

Angelfish fun facts:

Angelfish live in tropical waters near coral reefs. Young angelfish sometimes work as cleaning fish eating parasites from other fish. If a male angelfish is removed from the group, one of the females will turn into a male angelfish.

41

Sea turtle drawn by Kai Gabriel Szmidt, age 6

Sea turtle fun facts:

Sea turtles are air-breathing reptiles. Sea turtles do not have teeth. Sea turtle jaws have beaks so they can eat their food. Sea turtles live in the ocean and swim near land. Momma sea turtles come to shore to lay their eggs in the sand.

References for sea animal fun facts:

http://en.wikipedia.org/wiki/Butterfly

http://www.uky.edu/Ag/Horticulture/butterflypages/butterflyinfo.htm#Butterfly%20life

http://www.dolphins-world.com

http://animals.nationalgeographic.com/animals/fish/pufferfish

http://animals.nationalgeographic.com/animals/fish/sea-horse

http://animals.nationalgeographic.com/animals/fish/stingray

http://animals.nationalgeographic.com/animals/invertebrates/sea-anemone

http://animals.nationalgeographic.com/animals/fish/clown-anemonefish

http://animals.nationalgeographic.com/animals/invertebrates/lobster

http://animals.nationalgeographic.com/animals/fish/hammerhead-shark

http://animals.nationalgeographic.com/animals/invertebrates/common-octopus

http://animals.nationalgeographic.com/animals/invertebrates/box-jellyfish

http://animals.nationalgeographic.com/animals/invertebrates/starfish

http://www.ehow.com/facts_5612933_ocean-shrimp.html

http://www.aquaticcommunity.com/Marine-angelfish

http://www.conserveturtles.org/about.php

Made in the USA
Charleston, SC
19 July 2013